Trains for Kids

A Children's Picture Book about Trains

A Great Simple Picture Book for Kids to Learn about Different Types of Trains

Melissa Ackerman

PUBLISHED BY:

Melissa Ackerman

Copyright © 2016

All rights reserved.

No part of this publication may be copied, reproduced in any format, by any means, electronic or otherwise, without prior consent from the copyright owner and publisher of this book.

Disclaimer

The information contained in this book is for general information purposes only. The information is provided by the authors and while we endeavor to keep the information up to date and correct, we make no representations or warranties of any kind, express or implied, about the completeness, accuracy, reliability, suitability or availability with respect to the book or the information, products, services, or related graphics contained in the book for any purpose. Any reliance you place on such information is therefore strictly at your own risk.

TABLE OF CONTENTS

20th Century Limited 7

Acela Express 8

Adirondack 9

Afrosiyob Train 10

AGV 11

Ajanta Express 12

Al-Andalus 13

Alfa Pendular 14

Andean Explorer 15

Argo Bromo Anggrek 16

Atlantic Coast Express 17

Belmond British Pullman 18

Bernina Express 19

Black Diamond Express 20

Blue Ridge 21

Blue Water 22

Boxcar 23

Caledonian Sleeper 24

Capitol Corridor 25

Cascade 26

Catalan Talgo 27

Challenger 28

Coast Starlight 29

Cornishman 30

Coronation Scot 31

Deccan Odyssey 32

Desert Wind 33

E5 Series Shinkansen Hayabusa 34

Eastern & Oriental Express 35

El Transcantábrico 36

Electroliners 37

Empire Builder 38

Endeavour 39

ETR 500 Frecciarossa 40

Euroduplex 41

Eurostar e320 42

Flying Scotsman 43

FrontRunner 44

Glacier Discovery 45

Glacier Express 46

Golden Arrow 47

Golden Eagle Trans-Siberian Express 48

Gottardo 49

Gulflander 50

Green Diamond 51

Harmony CRH 380A 52

Hakutaka 53

Heartland Flyer 54

Helvetia 55

Hoosier State 56

Indian Pacific 57

Inter-American 58

Kingston Flyer 59

Maharajas' Express 60

Maple Leaf 61

Metroliner 62

Mizuho 63

Nakhon Phing Express 64

Napa Valley Wine Train 65

Nebraska Zephyr 66

Newcastle Flyer 67

Night Riviera 68

North Star 69

Nozomi 70

Open Wagon 71

Orange Blossom Special	72
Pride of Africa	73
Railjet	74
Refrigerated Boxcar	75
Rocky Mountaineer	76
Royal Canadian Pacific	77
Royal Scot	78
Sapsan	79
Seven Stars in Kyushu	80
Shanghai Maglev	81
Shangri-La Express	82
Siemens Velaro E	83
SNCF TGV Duplex	84
Super Chief	85
Talgo 350	86
TGV	87
Thalys	88
The Blue Train	89
The Bristolian	90
The Chips	91
The Coronation	92
The Ghan	93
The Gippslander	94
The Midlander	95
The Overland	96
The Red Dragon	97
THSR 700T	98
TranzAlpine	99
Tren Crucero	100
Troop Sleeper	101
Twin Cities Hiawatha	102
Venice Simplon-Orient-Express (VSOE)	103
Voralpen Express	104
Z-TER	105

20th Century Limited

The 20th Century Limited is an express passenger train or a train that has passenger-carrying capabilities. It operated from 1902 to 1967. Being an express train, it makes only a few stops throughout the entire journey. The 20th Century Limited was also considered as "The Most Famous Train in the World", travelling between Grand Central Terminal (GCT) in New York City and LaSalle Street Station in Chicago, Illinois. One of the most notable characteristics of this particular train is that it has a custom made red carpet where passengers can walk on to as they enter and exit the train.

Acela Express

The Acela Express or simply, Acela is a high speed train operated by Amtrak, an American passenger railroad service. It travels between Washington DC and Boston, Massachusetts with 14 stops all throughout a single journey. This train is considered as the fastest in America with 150 miles per hour highest speed. Acela also uses a tilting technology that allows the train to travel at higher speeds on sharp curves without distressing passengers. In 2013 alone, Acela was able to serve more than 3.3 million passengers and achieved a total revenue of $530,820,821.

Adirondack

Adirondack is a passenger train from Amtrak. It operates daily between New York City, USA and Montreal, Canada. The whole 381 mile trip takes around 11 hours for the Adirondack to cover. Moreover, Adirondack is known as train 68 (when travelling from Montreal to New York) and as train 69 (when travelling from New York to Montreal). In 2012 alone, this particular train carried 132,000 passengers and achieved a total revenue of $6,748,333. It first entered public service on August 5, 1974.

Afrosiyob Train

The Afrosiyob Train is a high-speed train that connects the two largest cities in Uzbekistan – Tashkent and Samarkand. The 344-kilometre journey passes through four provinces: Tashkent, Sirdaryo, Jizzakh and Samarkand. It also operates seven days a week. Since it entered commercial service in October 8, 2011 the train operates only twice a week. However, in January 2012, the services were upgraded to five times a week and then daily since February 13, 2012. And, from the original two hours and thirty minutes total time, the travel time has been reduced to two hours and eight minutes on February 10, 2013.

AGV

The AGV or Automotrice à grande vitesse in French is a high-speed electric train from Alstom, a French multinational company. It is available in different configurations from seven to fourteen carriages that can accommodate 245 to 446 persons. The maximum speed of AGV is 220 miles per hour. It also has an overall train length of 132.11 meters (7 carriages), width at around 2.99 meters and floor height at 1.16 meters. As of 2016, the only commercial order for the train was made by an Italian transport company named Nuovo Trasporto Viaggiatori (NTV). In 2008, NTV ordered 25 trains which entered services in 2012.

Ajanta Express

Ajanta Express is an Indian express train operated daily by South Central Railways, a railway zone in India. It travels from Secunderabad to Manmad or vice-versa, with a total of 21 stops in between. It has an average speed of 32 miles per hour. Ajanta Express is also available in different classes including: Air-conditioned Chair Car, Second Class seating, Sleeper Class and General Unreserved.

Al-Andalus

The Al Andalus is a European luxury train that has been originally used by the British Royal Family. It has high-class service, luxurious decoration, comfort and elegance. It has been considered as one of the most spacious and luxurious tourist trains in the world. The Al Andalus can also carry 64 passengers in its 12 Junior Suites and 20 Deluxe Suites. The Junior Suite has two twin beds, a safe, a minibar, a wardrobe and a directly attached bathroom. The Deluxe Suite on the other hand, has a double bed, a minibar, a safe, a wardrobe and a magnificent full bathroom. All these suites have air-conditioning and heating system and 220 volt sockets. All the beds can also be folded up into comfortable sofas. The journey on this particular train is from Seville, Spain. The train will then head to Jerez de la Frontera, Cadiz, Ronda, Granada and Cordoba (which are all cities in Spain) before going back to Seville.

Alfa Pendular

Alfa Pendular is a high-speed tilting train from Portugal. Tilting trains are trains that have a mechanism that enables it to run at high speed when passing on a curve without distressing the passengers on board. It was operated by the railway company Comboios de Portugal (Trains of Portugal) since 1999 and connects the cities of Braga, Porto, Aveiro, Coimbra, Santarém, Lisbon, Albufeira and Faro. It has a top speed of up to 152.6 miles per hour and is made up of six individual cars. It also has 301 seating capacity, 158.9 meters train length, 2.92 meters width, 4.39 meters height. In total, there are only 10 Alfa Pendular units built.

Andean Explorer

The Andean Explorer is the first luxury sleeper train in South America. It was scheduled for launching in May 2017. It will run along the world's highest rail routes from Cusco to Lake Titicaca and Arequipa in Peru. The usual trip will last for one or two nights passing through natural wonders and ancient kingdoms such as the Colca Canyon and the city center of Arequipa, a UNESCO World Heritage site.

Argo Bromo Anggrek

Argo Bromo Anggrek is an executive class train introduced in 24 September 1997. Executive class trains has more legroom, luggage space, has good outside view and has wider seats compared to ordinary passenger trains. It is operated twice daily by PT Kereta Api Indonesia (major operator of public railways in Indonesia) and travels between Jakarta and Surabaya with a total of 4 stops. The 725 kilometers distance between the two endpoints can be covered in 9 hours by the Argo Bromo Anggrek. Moreover, this particular train is composed of 5 to 7 executive class passenger carriages which are white in color with green stripes along the sides. Furthermore, Argo Bromo Anggrek features a restaurant carriage where passengers can order food and drinks and even enjoy karaoke.

Atlantic Coast Express

The Atlantic Coast Express or ACE is an express passenger train. It operated from 1926 to 1964 and was re-launched in 2008 by First Great Western. Today, it operates between Paddington station, London, and Newquay. Because the number of passengers greatly increases during holidays, about five Atlantic Coast Express trains operate every Saturdays during summer. However, during winter, only one train operates.

Belmond British Pullman

Belmond British Pullman is a private luxury train. It was owned by Belmond Ltd and operates around London, making visits on several tourist spots like castles, country houses, sporting occasions and events like the Grand National (horse race) and Goodwood Revival (car and motorcycle race). It also offers weekend journeys, with overnight accommodation in hotels, and non-stop round trips with lunch, tea and dinner served on board.

Bernina Express

Bernina Express is a "tourist-favorite" train operated by the Rhaetian Railway, a Swiss transport company. It travels between Chur in Switzerland and Poschiavo and Tirano in Italy. It crosses the Swiss Engadin Alps and also runs along the Albula / Bernina Landscapes, a site considered as a World Heritage Site. Bernina Express is specifically built for sightseeing purposes; hence, it has enlarged windows, multi-lingual audio guide on board and a minibar.

Black Diamond Express

Black Diamond Express is a super-fast mail-express train or a train that makes very few stops compared to passenger train, hence, achieving shorter journey times. It is being operated by Indian Railways (an Indian state-owned enterprise) since 1 July 2013. It travels between Kolkata and the towns of Raniganj, Asansol, Kulti, Durgapur, Dhanbad. The Tatkal scheme or booking journeys at very short notice is available in this particular train. It also doesn't have a pantry car or a restaurant-like carriage that serves meals. The Black Diamond Express is also considered an important train as it operates during office hours. Furthermore, its average operating speed is around 35 miles per hour.

Blue Ridge

The Blue Ridge is a passenger train operated daily by Amtrak, with operation starting on May 7, 1973 and ending in 1986. It travels between Washington, D.C. and Martinsburg, West Virginia with five stops in between each trip. The distance between the two end points is about 74 miles and it will take only 1 hour and 40 minutes for the Blue Ridge to cover the distance.

Blue Water

The Blue Water is another high-speed passenger train operated daily by Amtrak since April 25, 2004. It connects Port Huron, Michigan and Chicago, Illinois, with a total of 319 miles distance. In the year 2013 alone, it was able to service 191,106 passengers and achieved total revenue of $5.8 million.

Boxcar

A boxcar is an enclosed railroad car from North America. It has an enclosed body and is typically used to carry different cargos. It is considered as a versatile vehicle as it can carry most types of loads like coal, grain, livestock, supplies, workers and even military troops and war prisoners during the World War II. These Boxcars have differently sized side doors and often times end doors to ease the loading and unloading of cargos.

Caledonian Sleeper

Caledonian Sleepers are overnight sleeper trains travelling between London and Scotland. It is being operated by Serco Caledonian Sleepers Limited, every night, except Saturday night. It typically runs at a maximum speed of 80 miles per hour, however, when the train has been delayed for more than 20 minutes, it can run for about 100 miles per hour. In total, a single Caledonian Sleeper is composed of 75 carriages.

Capitol Corridor

The Capitol Corridor is a passenger train operating since December 1991by Capitol Corridor Joint Powers Authority, in partnership with Amtrak and Caltrans. It runs between San Jose and Sacramento in California, with a total of 168 miles distance. In average, the average journey of a Capital Corridor lasts for up to 3 hours and15 minutes.

Cascade

The Cascade is a passenger train operated by Amtrak in partnership with the U.S. states of Washington and Oregon and the Canadian province of British Columbia. Its name was derived from the Cascade mountain range that can be seen throughout the train journey. It travels the 467 miles distance between Vancouver, British Columbia and Eugene, Oregon. As of December 2011 four Cascades operate daily. In the year 2015 alone, this particular train was able to serve 744,000 passengers and achieve a total revenue of $29,932,876.

Catalan Talgo

The Catalan Talgo is an international express train operating since 1969. It connects Geneva, Switzerland with Barcelona, Spain. It also has generator cars located on both ends which are the source of the train's electrical power. One of these generator cars has the train chief's office, while the other, serves as a luggage compartment. In between the two generator cars, nine carriages are available: one kitchen car, two dining cars and nine cars for passengers.

Challenger

The Challenger is an economy class (lowest travel class of seating) passenger train that travel between Chicago, Illinois and the West Coast of the United States. This steam train was specifically designed to try to draw people from the Depression-Era (a severe worldwide economic depression in the 1930s) back to the rails. It also offers a budget-friendly food service. Because of its affordability, the Challenger became the most-patronized train, achieving the highest revenue compared to other American trains. However, in 1947, this particular train was discontinued.

Coast Starlight

The Coast Starlight is a passenger train that travels between Seattle, Washington to Los Angeles, California. It was operated by Amtrak since May 1, 1971 and was considered as the first train to connect the two cities. It is a very unique train from Amtrak as it includes a first-class lounge car called the "Pacific Parlour Car". This particular carriage is a double-decker car which is about 4.7 m high. The whole upper level is for the passengers, while the lower level includes the restrooms and baggage areas. It also features a central staircase and a row of windows across the upper level.

Cornishman

The Cornishman is an express passenger train that originated in London. It first operates in 1890 between London Paddington and Penzance in Cornwall. It was also considered as one of the most popular and fastest trains in the West of England. However, in July 1904, a new express train called Cornish Riviera Limited replaced the Cornishman. The Cornishman was then reintroduced in 1935, but was again removed from service in 1936. Fortunately, in 2006, the Great Western Railway (British train operating company) began to use the Cornishman once again, still travelling between London Paddington and Penzance.

Coronation Scot

The Coronation Scot is an express passenger train launched in 1937 for the coronation of King George VI and Queen Elizabeth. Its operation ended in 1939 just before the World War I. It travels between London and Glasgow in 6 hours 30 minutes on weekdays and during summer weekends. The five trains produced are blue in color with silver lines, while the next fifteen units are red with gold lines.

Deccan Odyssey

The Deccan Odyssey is a special luxury train based on Palace on Wheels, a luxury tourist train. It is a joint project of the Maharashtra Government and the Ministry of Railways, Government of India. It was specifically designed to boost tourism on the Maharashtra route of the Indian Railways. Its journey starts in Mumbai and then to the different cities in Maharashtra, India and back to Mumbai. Aside from visiting different tourist spots, the Deccan Odyssey is also like a 5-star hotel on wheels that features special amenities like two restaurants, a bar, a sauna and a business center. Starting December 2010, the Deccan Odyssey offers a 7-nights journey across the five Sikh takhts or Five Holy Takhats, which are the places of worship for the Sikhism religion.

Desert Wind

The Desert Wind is a long distance passenger train operating from 1979 to 1997. It was operated by Amtrak and travels from Los Angeles, California to Ogden, Utah. In 1983, it was renamed California Zephyr and begins to travel between Emeryville, California and Chicago, Illinois. The whole 2,397 miles travel takes about 48 hours and 30 minutes for the California Zephyr to cover. Its on-board facilities include: catering facilities, a dining car, a café and a sightseer lounge.

E5 Series Shinkansen Hayabusa

The E5 series Shinkansen Hayabusa is considered as the fastest train in Japan today. It was first introduced in March 2011 and was operated by the East Japan railway company. It travels between Tokyo and Aomory in just 2 hours and 56 minutes at a top speed of 320 kilometers per hour. The front end of this train has a 15 meter long nose that helps minimize the sound and vibration as the train travels through tunnels. It is composed of 10 car sets and can seat up to 731 passengers. It also offers three seating classes including: standard (658 seats), green (55 seats) and gran class (18 seats). The gran class is the main attraction of Hayabusa train that offers high end luxury facilities such as, eye mask, slippers, blankets, soft drinks and food.

Eastern & Oriental Express

The Eastern & Oriental Express is a luxury train operated by Belmond Ltd., a hotel and leisure company. It features two dining cars, with tables that seat two or four persons. It also has a library car, a saloon car for overflow dining and two bar cars, one of which has an open-air observation deck. The train, as well, is fully air-conditioned with all the facilities of a luxury 5 star hotel. In addition, Eastern & Oriental Express offers different accommodations: two Presidential Suites (most expensive), Staterooms (2nd most expensive) and Pullman compartments (the cheapest). This particular train travels between Singapore and Thailand. The 1,262 miles trip usually lasts for four days and three nights. It also runs several times a month most of the year. As of September 2015 the fare for Eastern & Oriental Express starts at US$2,690. Moreover, since 2007 the train also offers travel between Bangkok and Laos.

El Transcantábrico

The El Transcantábrico is a luxury train from Northern Spain that entered service in 1983. It travels between Leon, Spain and Santiago de Compostela, Spain. It can accommodate 52 passengers on its six sleeper cars, each with four double cabins. In May 2011, the El Transcantábrico offered a new luxury service called the Gran Lujo. The Gran Lujo has Preferente Suites which have a total area of 129 square feet. The Preferente Suites also offers a double bed, long sofa, flat-screen DVD, computer and lots of storage. However, with the Gran Lujo service, the train can only take 28 passengers for a much more intimate travel experience.

Electroliners

Electroliners were a pair of four-coach electric interurban passenger train or streetcar-like electric train that runs within and between cities or towns. It was operated by the Chicago North Shore and Milwaukee Railroad, an interurban railroad line. It traveled between Chicago, Illinois and Milwaukee, Wisconsin from 1941 to 1976. In total, there were only two electric units built, which were both preserved at the Rockhill Trolley Museum in Orbisonia, Pennsylvania.

Empire Builder

The Empire Builder is a passenger train operated daily by Amtrak. It was considered as Amtrak's busiest long-distance train that runs in two routes: Chicago to Portland and Chicago to Seattle. When the train reached Spokane, Washington, the Empire Builder will split into two: one part will travel to Portland, while the other part will go straight to Seattle. The entire trip which is about 2,206-2,257 miles long takes about 45 to 46 hours to cover.

Endeavour

The Endeavour is a long-distance passenger train that operated from 1972 to 1989. It travels between Wellington and Napier in New Zealand. It has five passenger carriages and a buffet car (removed in August 8, 1981). Three of the five passenger cars can seat 36 persons each, while the last two cars can seat 32 passengers each. Later on, a sixth second class car (can seat 32) was added to accommodate more passengers.

ETR 500 Frecciarossa

The ETR 500 Frecciarossa is the fastest train in Italy. It was operated by Trenitalia Company and travels between Milan and Rome in just 2 hours and 40 minutes at a maximum speed of 300 kilometers per hour. It was also built by three manufacturing companies: AnsaldoBreda (from Italy), Bombardier (from Canada) and Alstom (from France). The Frecciarossa also offers four main seating classes: standard class, premium class, business class and executive class. All of these are sound proof and offer free Wi-Fi.

Euroduplex

The Euroduplex is a high speed double deck train operated since December 2011 by SNCF, a French railway company. It was designed and built by the Alstom railway company. It connects the French, Swiss, German and Luxembourg rail networks. It can also travel at a top speed of 320 kilometers per hour and can carry about 1020 passengers in a single journey. The Euroduplex also features electric sockets and real time travel information screen near the door and inside the carriages.

Eurostar e320

The Eurostar e320 or Class 374 is an electric high speed train owned by Eurostar International Limited, a railway company from London. It was intended for use through the Channel Tunnel, a rail tunnel that runs beneath the English Channel, the body of water that separates southern England from northern France. It specifically connects the United Kingdom with northern France. It started its service in December 2015. It has 16 carriages and can seat 902 passengers. In total, there are six Eurostart e320 units produced and 11 units which are still under construction.

Flying Scotsman

The Flying Scotsman is an express luxury passenger train that travels between Edinburgh, Scotland and London, England since 1862. It is being operated by Virgin Trains East Coast, a train operating company in the United Kingdom. The Flying Scotsman also offers different amenities such as, hairdressing salon, a high-end restaurant and bar and a cinema coach.

FrontRunner

The FrontRunner is a passenger train owned by the Utah Transit Authority (UTA), the provider of public transportation across the Wasatch Front of Utah. Since April 26, 2008, the train takes passengers through an 88-mile journey from Pleasant View in northern Weber County to Provo in central Utah County. As of March 2016 the base fare for FrontRunner is $2.50, with an additional $0.60 for each additional stop and maximum fare reaching up to $10.30. The estimated number of passengers that get on-board FrontRunner is about 16,800.

Glacier Discovery

The Glacier Discovery is a passenger train that connects the towns of Anchorage, Whittier Alaska and the rail station known as Grandview. It is operated by the Alaska Railroad, a railroad company from Alaska. The Glacier Discovery is considered as a seasonal train, operating daily only from May to September. The entire 68.7 miles trip between the two end points usually takes about two hours (average) to cover.

Glacier Express

The Glacier Express is an express train that connects the two major mountain resorts of St. Moritz and Zermatt in the Swiss Alps. It was operated by two railway and transport companies from Switzerland named Matterhorn Gotthard Bahn (MGB) and Rhaetian Railway (RhB). It was also considered as the world's slowest express train, travelling the entire 168 mountainous miles journey for almost eight hours. Furthermore, the Glacier Express passes across 291 bridges, 91 tunnels and across the Oberalp Pass, a high mountain pass in the Swiss Alps. The windows of this particular train can also be opened so passengers can fully enjoy and photograph the fantastic scenery.

Golden Arrow

The Golden Arrow is a luxury boat train or a passenger train that travels to a port for the specific purpose of taking its passengers to a ferry or ocean liner. It is operated first by Southern Railway and then by British Railways. It connects London with Dover, a port in England where passengers took the ferry to Calais, a port in Northern France to get on-board another train that will take them to Paris. The entire trip (from London to Dover) typically lasts for 80 minutes. However, due to a decline in demand for rail travel between London and Paris, the Golden Arrow had its last run on September 30, 1972. Today, this particular train is being preserved in Sussex, a historic county in South East England.

Golden Eagle Trans-Siberian Express

The Golden Eagle Trans-Siberian Express is a luxury train introduced in April 2007. It travels on a 6,000 miles journey which has been considered as the world's longest train journey. The whole journey passes across two continents and eight time zones. It connects Moscow and European Russia with the Russian provinces, Mongolia, China and the Sea of Japan. It also offers different accommodations such as, Imperial Suite, Gold Class and Silver Class, all with directly-attached bathroom. The new Imperial Suites offer a fixed king-sized bed, a dedicated dressing table and lounge area. The Golden Eagle Trans-Siberian Express, additionally, has two dining cars and a lounge car.

Gottardo

The Gottardo is an express train that travels the 293 km distance between Zurich, Switzerland and Milan, Italy. It runs along the Gotthard railway, hence, the name. It first entered service in July 1, 1961 as a first-class-only train until 1988. However, since 1988 this particular train started offering first class and second class accommodation. It also features a restaurant car that serves decent meals to passengers. In June 15, 2002 the use of Gottardo trains was discontinued.

Gulflander

The Gulflander is an Australian passenger train operated by Queensland Rail, a state owned railway company in Queensland, Australia. It travels through a 151 km journey between Normanton to Croydon in northern Queensland. It entered service on 1891. It usually runs once a week to Croydon on Wednesdays and then returns to Normanton on Thursdays. On the remaining days, the Gulflander can be charted or rented for shorter travels. However, today, this particular train serves as a tourist attraction, with train crews qualified as tour guides. The train usually stops on tourist spots and the crews/guides will talk about it.

Green Diamond

The Green Diamond is passenger train operated by the Illinois Central Railroad, a railroad company from the United States. Its name honored the "green diamond" in the company's logo and the company's oldest train on the Chicago-St. Louis run, the Diamond Special. It travels between Chicago, Illinois and St. Louis, Missouri from 1936 to 1968. The entire 294 miles journey typically takes 4 hours and 55 minutes to cover.

Harmony CRH 380A

The Harmony CRH 380A is considered as the second fastest train in the world. It is operated by China railways and first introduced in October 2010. It run between Shanghai and Nanjing in China and can travel at a maximum speed of 380 kilometers per hour. It was able to achieve a speed of 416.6 kilometers per hour during initial tests before it entered public service. It has a lightweight body and a front end which resembles a fish head. It also has a 494 seating capacity and offers other facilities like, reading lamps, power ports and an electronic display. Moreover, the Harmony CRH 380A also has a VIP sightseeing area near the driver's cabin and a carriage dedicated for serving food and drinks for passengers.

Hakutaka

The Hakutaka or "White hawk" in English is a high-speed train operated by East Japan Railway Company (JR East) and West Japan Railway Company (JR West), major passenger railway companies in Japan. It travels between Tokyo and Kanazawa. Since its introduction on March 14, 2015, the Hakutaka operates daily with a maximum operating speed of 260 kilometers per hour. The first 10 cars of this particular train are ordinary-class cars with 2+3 seating configuration (two seats on one side, three seats on the other side), the 11th car is a "Green" car with 2+2 seating configuration, and the 12th car is a "Gran Class" car with 2+1 seating. All these cars are strictly no-smoking.

Heartland Flyer

The Heartland Flyer is a passenger train operated by Amtrak since June 14, 1999. It travels daily on the 206-mile route from Oklahoma City, Oklahoma to Fort Worth, Texas. As of November 2007, this particular train already carried a total of 500,000 passengers since its launching. And in November 2013, the train carried its millionth passenger. Moreover, this particular train is unique because it is connected to and allows transfers of passengers to another train. The Heartland Flyer is connected to the Texas Eagle train that runs daily between Chicago, Illinois and San Antonio, Texas and continues three days each week to Los Angeles, California. It is also connected to the Trinity Railway Express which runs from Fort Worth to nearby Dallas from Monday through Saturday each week.

Helvetia

The Helvetia is an express train operated by the companies, Deutsche Bundesbahn / Deutsche Bahn (DB), from Germany and the Swiss Federal Railways (SBB-CFF-FFS), from Switzerland. Its name was derived for the Latin word for "Switzerland". It connects Hamburg, Germany with Zurich, Switzerland since its introduction in 1952. The service of this particular train ended in 2002.

Hoosier State

The Hoosier State is a passenger train owned by Amtrak. It travels on a 196-mile route from Chicago to Indianapolis since October 1, 1980. It operates four days a week: leaving Chicago on Sunday, Monday, Wednesday, and Friday; leaving Indianapolis on Sunday, Tuesday, Wednesday, and Friday. In the year 2011 alone, this particular train carried around 37,000 passengers and was able to reach total revenue of $836,057.

Indian Pacific

The Indian Pacific is a first-class train that offers twice-weekly service in Australia, between Perth and Sydney, via Adelaide. The journey is about 2,704 miles long, 300 miles of which crosses the Nullarbor Plain which was considered as the longest straight track in the world. The entire trip in Indian Pacific takes three nights. Travelers especially enjoy and get on-board this particular train around holiday periods.

Inter-American

The Inter-American is a passenger train operated by Amtrak since January 27, 1973, connecting Laredo with Fort Worth. However, in March 1974, the train was extended to St. Louis and then all the way to Dallas. In October 1976, the route changes again and the train service was extended to Chicago. The train between Chicago and St. Louis operated daily, while the train between St. Louis and Laredo operated thrice a week. Unfortunately, on October 1, 1981 the Inter-American has been discontinued and was replaced by Texas Eagle.

Kingston Flyer

The Kingston Flyer is a steam train in New Zealand. A steam train is a train powered by a steam engine. Originally, it was a passenger express train operated by New Zealand Railways Department, a government department in-charged with New Zealand's railway. From the 1890s to 1957, it used to travel between Kingston, Gore, Invercargill, and Dunedin.

Maharajas' Express

The Maharajas' Express is an 84-passenger luxury tourist train owned by Indian Railway Catering and Tourism Corporation. It passes through five different routes: Indian Splendor Route (Delhi - Agra - Ranthambore - Jaipur - Bikaner - Jodhpur - Udaipur - Balasinor - Mumbai); Indian Panorama Route (Delhi - Jaipur - Ranthambore - Fatehpur Sikri - Agra - Gwalior - Orchha - Khajuraho - Varanasi - Lucknow - Delhi); Heritage of India Route (Mumbai - Ajanta - Udaipur - Jodhpur - Bikaner - Jaipur - Ranthambore - Agra - Delhi); Treasures of India Route (Delhi - Agra - Ranthambore - Jaipur - Delhi) and; Gems of India Route (Delhi - Agra - Ranthambore - Jaipur - Delhi). It was also voted as "The World's Leading Luxury Train" four times in a row (2012 to 2015). It has been considered as Asia's most expensive luxury train. Designed to be the most luxurious train in India, the Maharajas' Express offers one-of-a-kind facilities and amenities. All its cabins have large windows, free wi-fi, temperature controls, LCD televisions, and private bathrooms. It also has a single exclusive Presidential Suite which is the largest suite available on any train in the world. Moreover, the Maharajas' Express has elegantly decorated dining cars and two lounge cars.

Maple Leaf

The Maple Leaf is an international passenger train that connects Pennsylvania Station in New York City and Union Station in Toronto, Canada since 1981. It is being operated daily by Amtrak and Via Rail, an independent state-owned company. The entire 544-mile journey takes about 12 hours to cover.

Metroliner

The Metroliner is an extra-fare express train first operated by Penn Central Transportation and then by Amtrak. It connects Washington, D.C., and New York City for about 2.5 to 3.4 hours. The Metroliner served passengers from 1969 to 2000s, until it was replaced by Acela Express. It offered both business-class and first-class accommodation.

Mizuho

The Mizuho ("abundant rice" or "harvest") is a limited-stop high-speed train operated by JR West. It connects Shin-Osaka and Kagoshima-Chuo in Japan since 12 March 2011. Originally, the Mizuho was first introduced on October 1, 1961 as a seasonal limited express sleeper train. During those times, it ran from Tokyo to Kumamoto in Kyushu. After a year, the service was upgraded from seasonal to a daily service. And in December 3, 1994 the Mizuho service was discontinued. It was not until March 2011 that this particular train was used again.

Nakhon Phing Express

Nakhon Phing Express is an express train owned by the State Railway of Thailand. It travels between Bangkok and Chiang Mai. There are two Nakhon Phing Express units built - one travels from Bangkok to Chiang Mai, while the other one travels from Chiang Mai to Bangkok. It also offers first class and second class sleeping cars and a restaurant car. It was first introduced in April 13, 1987, with the entire 467 miles journey lasting for 13 hours in average. The maximum operating speed for Nakhon Phing Express is 90 kilometers per hour.

Napa Valley Wine Train

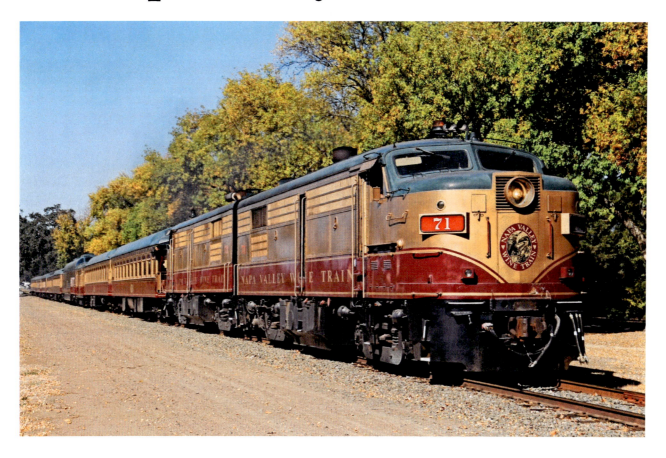

The Napa Valley Wine Train is an excursion train (train run/rented for a special event or purpose) that connects Napa, California and St. Helena, California. The 36-mile trip typically lasts for three hours. It is being operated by the Napa Valley Railroad, a private company owned by the DeDomenico family. This train has been in service since September 16, 1989 and has carried more than 2 million passengers. It has a maximum capacity of 370 passengers and usually runs twice a day. On the trip, passengers can enjoy a gourmet meal available on board and can also sample local wines available in one of the lounge cars. In June 1, 2016 a new service called the Quattro Vino was offered. The new service will make the Napa Valley Wine Train drop off and pick up passengers at four wineries: Robert Mondavi winery, Charles Krug winery, Merryvale winery and V. Sattui winery. This new service is a six hour tour that operates only once per day.

Nebraska Zephyr

The Nebraska Zephyr is a passenger train that runs between Chicago, Illinois, Omaha, Nebraska and Lincoln, Nebraska. It was operated by the Chicago, Burlington and Quincy Railroad from 1947 to 1971. There are two original Nebraska Zephyr trains that operated, the "Train of the Gods" and "Train of the Goddesses". And when the service of this particular train was discontinued, the "Train of the Goddess" has been preserved at the Illinois Railway Museum in Union, Illinois.

Newcastle Flyer

The Newcastle Flyer is a passenger express train in Australian. It was operated by State Rail Authority of New South Wales from 1929 to 1988. It travels between Sydney and Newcastle in Australia. It runs the 168 kilometers trip thrice a day in each direction. Moreover, the Newcastle Flyer became famous for its speed and high level of comfort provided to passengers. However, since 1985 the carriage sets of this train were reduced from seven to five carriages. And on March 1986, the first class accommodation was removed.

Night Riviera

The Night Riviera is one of the two sleeper trains in the United Kingdom (the other one is the Caledonian Sleeper). It was operated by Great Western Railway and runs about six nights a week, from Sunday to Friday between London Paddington and Penzance. Only one train operates in each direction. It has 10 sleeping carriages and 8 seating carriages. All these carriages are fully air-conditioned. Aside from the standard fare, passengers can avail a fixed bed (for sleeping) that comes with a supplementary charge.

North Star

The North Star is a passenger train operated by Amtrak from 1978 to 1985. It originally travels between Chicago, Illinois and Duluth, Minnesota (1978 - 1981). However, the route was soon changed and the train started travelling between Saint Paul, Minnesota and Duluth, Minnesota (1981 - 1985).

Nozomi

The Nozomi (meaning "hope" or "wish") is a high-speed train in Japan. It was operated by JR west and connects Tokyo and Osaka with a distance of 515 kilometers. It can reach a speed of 300 kilometers per hour, making the entire trip to last only for 2 hours and 22 minutes. A total of 16 seating carriages make up the train, all of which are air-conditioned except for the smoking area carriages.

Open Wagon

Open wagons are railway wagons designed to transport bulk cargos. The usual cargos carried by this vehicle are those that can be tipped, dumped or shoveled. Open wagons have two major classes: the ordinary and the special. Ordinary open wagons feature a level floor, solid sides and at least one door on each side. These types of open wagons are typically used to carry steel, scrap, coal, wood and paper. Special open wagons on the other hand are capable of discharging the goods they carry on their own. The self-discharge operation can be done through different ways: side-tipping, by the use of a discharge chute or a conveyor belt and by using a mechanism that will flap the sides out and slope the floor downward to dump its load.

Orange Blossom Special

The Orange Blossom Special is a deluxe passenger train that connects New York City and Miami. It only operates during the winter season. Its service started on November 21, 1925, running only from New York to West Palm Beach. It wasn't until 1927 that the train was able to reach Miami. The Orange Blossom Special also became famous for its speed and luxury. During World War II the service of this particular train was suspended so it can be used in transporting military troops. And in 1953, the Orange Blossom Special had its last run. However, plans are being made to restore the train so it can be used again for eventual excursion service.

Pride of Africa

The Pride of Africa is a luxury train operated by Rovos Rail, a private railway company in South Africa. It travels through South Africa, Zimbabwe, Zambia and Tanzania. It was considered as one of the world's most luxurious trains as it offers exceptional elegance, luxury and dining experience. Pride of Africa also features three different accommodations that guests can choose from: Royal Suites, which have a private lounge area and a full directly-attached bathroom with shower and bath tub; Deluxe Suites, a smaller room with a lounge area and a bathroom with shower; and Pullman Suites, the smallest room with a sofa-seat that can be converted to double or twin beds for the evening and a bathroom with shower. There is also a mini bar filled with beverages of the passengers' choice and 24 hour room service.

Railjet

The Railjet is a high-speed train operated by Austrian Federal Railways (the national railway system of Austria) and Czech Railways (the main railway operator in the Czech Republic). Commercial services of this train between Munich, Vienna and Budapest started on December 14, 2008. While in December 2009, the service started between Vienna and Zürich and Bregenz. It also operates within Austria and on nearby countries such as, Czech Republic, Germany, Switzerland, Hungary, and from December 2016 Italy. The Railjet runs at a maximum speed of up to 230 kilometers per hour.

Refrigerated Boxcar

A refrigerator car or a reefer is a refrigerated boxcar especially designed to carry perishable goods. It is fitted with a cooling apparatus to keep its loads on a specific temperature. It can be cooled by using a mechanical refrigeration system or dry ice as a cooling agent. Typically, refrigerated cars are utilized for goods with less than 14 days life such as, cut flowers, green leafy vegetables, fruits, meat products, mushrooms, human blood, fish, green onions, milk, and some pharmaceutical supplies.

Rocky Mountaineer

The Rocky Mountaineer is a double deck first-class passenger train in Canada. It is undeniably comfortable and classy with its custom-built glass dome coaches. It offers fine dining on the lower level with local wines and outdoor viewing area on the rear end of the train. In total, the Rocky Mountaineer has four routes: Vancouver to Banff and Calgary, Vancouver to Jasper via Kamloops, Vancouver to Jasper via Quesnel and Vancouver to Seattle.

Royal Canadian Pacific

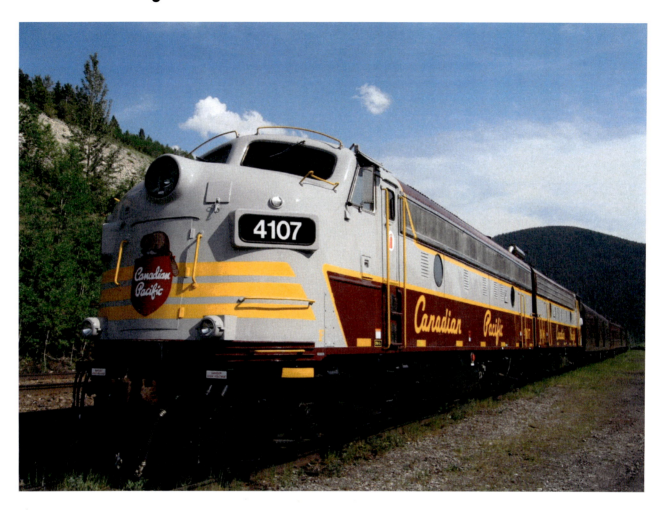

The Royal Canadian Pacific is the most luxurious train in North America. It is being offered exclusively as a whole-train charter or for private use only. It was launched on June 7, 2000 after it received the royal designation from Queen Elizabeth II, Queen of Canada, when she got on-board on one of its carriages. It operates seasonally from June to September at a typical 650 miles distance from Calgary to Columbia River Valley and Crowsnest Pass and then back to Calgary. The trip usually takes six days and five nights. However, the Royal Canadian Pacific does not operate at night so passengers can enjoy the scenery. Additionally, it can accommodate up to 30 persons who are treated like royalty in this particular train. It offers an on-board five-star dining, open-platform observation areas and small salons. It also features elegant musical events and large compartments that have private shower, toilet and sink.

Royal Scot

The Royal Scot is an express passenger train from Great Britain that connects London Euston and Glasgow Central. It first operates in 1862, with trains departing from both ends at 10:00 in the morning. It also usually has 15 coaches, a total length of about 230 yards and can accommodate around 290 passengers. Today, the Royal Scot still operates on the strike of 10:00 (morning). At night, the train will gently get slower and slower until it stops, on time, at its destination.

Sapsan

The Sapsan or Velaro RUS EVS is a high-speed electric express train operated by the Russian company named Russian Railways. It entered service in December 2009 and started travelling in two routes: Moscow - Saint Petersburg and Moscow - Nizhniy Novgorod. It usually operates at a maximum speed of 250 kilometers per hour. It is also made up of 10 cars and can accommodate up to 604 passengers.

Seven Stars in Kyushu

The Seven Stars in Kyushu is a deluxe excursion train or train rented for a special event or purpose. It was operated by Kyushu Railway Company in Japan. Since its launching in October 2013, the Seven Stars in Kyushu has been considered as Japan's very first luxury train. It has a lounge car, dining cars and fourteen cabins. The service of this particular train is unique as it does not only take its passengers on a journey. At certain points, passengers will get off from the train and participate in excursions.

Shanghai Maglev

Shanghai Maglev is considered as the fastest train in the whole world. It was operated by Shanghai Maglev Transportation Development Co. and started its public service on January 1, 2004, connecting Shanghai Pudong International Airport and the outskirts of central Pudong in just 7 minutes and 20 seconds. It has a maximum speed of 431 kilometers per hour and runs at Shanghai's high speed magnetic levitation (Maglev) line where the train moves without touching the ground. In other words, the Shanghai Maglev doesn't have wheels – it floats or literally flies over the track with the help of a magnetic field between the train and track. It also has a total of 574 passenger capacity and a ticket cost of US$8 (standard) and US$16 for VIP ticket.

Shangri-La Express

The Shangri-La Express is a private first-class train. It was considered as the most modern hotel train in China. It offers comfort and amazing shower cars that has spacious area for changing. These shower cars which are considered as the most modern shower cars have water that is as strong as that in a good hotel. The Shangri-La Express is also fully air-conditioned and has first-class sleeping cabins with two twin beds, a restaurant car, a bar car, free in-room fruit tray and daily room service. In addition, the Shangri-La Express travels in two routes: Silk Road (Eastbound) from Moscow, Russia to Beijing, China; Silk Road (Westbound) from Beijing, China to Moscow, Russia.

Siemens Velaro E

Siemens Velaro E (or AVS 103) is a high speed train developed by Siemens, a German engineering company. It is operated in Spain by the Spanish National Railways since June 2007. It connects Barcelona and Madrid in 2 hours and 30 minutes journey with its 350 kilometers per hour maximum speed. However, the Velaro E can also achieve a top speed of 403.7 kilometers per hour. This particular train is composed of 8 passenger cars and offers a seating capacity of 404.

SNCF TGV Duplex

The SNCF TGV Duplex is the fastest train in France. It is operated by SNCF Railway Company and launched in December 2011. It can run for up to 320 kilometers per hour and connects all major cities in France. TGV Duplex also has double-deck carriages and is considered as one of most comfortable European trains. It has a seating capacity of 508 and offers three main seating classes: standard class, first class and TGV Pro. The standard class has comfortable seats, snack vending machines and a bar buffet. The first class on the other has more comfortable reclining seats, individual reading lights and sockets for electrical devices. While the TGV Pro class offers extra comfortable and spacious seats, free Wi-Fi, a welcome drink, newspapers and magazines.

Super Chief

The Super Chief is a passenger train noted as "The Train of the Stars". This is because it has carried different celebrities between Chicago, Illinois, and Los Angeles, California. It originally runs once a week and then twice weekly beginning in 1938 and daily after 1948. The Super Chief was also renowned for its gourmet food and Hollywood clientele.

Talgo 350

Talgo 350 is a high speed train from Spain. It was operated by RENFE, a railway company run by the state of Spain. It connects Madrid and Barcelona and can reach a maximum speed of 350 kilometers per hour. In Spain, Talgo 350 is also known as 'Pato', referring to its front nose which looks like a duck's beak. It offers four different seating classes: Club class, First class, Bistro class and Coach class. All these classes have comfortable reclining seats with foot rests and video, audio devices.

TGV

TGV or Train à Grande Vitesse is a high-speed passenger train in France. It is operated by SNCF, a national rail operator. A TGV test train which was able to reach 574.8 km/h top speed has set the record for the fastest wheeled train. In 2011, TGV trains operated at 320 km/h speed, which was considered as the highest speed used by a conventional train service. Originally, it travels between Paris and Lyon in 1981. However, TGV train service become so successful that its operator decided to expand to connect main cities across France and in nearby countries. In comparison to other high-speed trains, TGV tickets cost way much lower.

Thalys

Thalys is an international high-speed train operated by the companies from Belgium named, THI Factory and SNCB. It travels between Paris and Brussels (since 1924) and then, between Lille Europe and Amsterdam Centraal (in 2014). However, at the end of March 2015, due to funding issues, the Paris to Brussels route was dropped. Soon enough, on March 30, 2015, Thalys became a train company (THI Factory) and operates under its own train operator certificate.

The Blue Train

The Blue Train is a luxury train from South Africa where kings and presidents have travelled on. It travels between Pretoria and Cape Town which is about 1,600-kilometer far from each other. It is noted as one of the most luxurious trains in the world with its butler service, an observation car, two lounge cars and sound-proofed, fully carpeted cabins. All of these cabins have their own private bathroom. Moreover, The Blue Train is being operated by Spoornet (a state-owned transport company) eight times a month in a 27-hour journey with sightseeing stop in between.

The Bristolian

The Bristolian is a passenger train running from London Paddington to Bristol Temple Meads. It was first introduced in 1935 by the Great Western Railway, a British train operating company. This train service is exceptional as its route takes it in an up and down directions. The up train is the one that came from Bristol as it will climb up the Ashley Hill Bank to be able to reach Bristol. On the other hand, the train departing Paddington is considered as the down train as the way to Bristol is in downward manner.

The Chips

The Chips is a passenger train operated daily by NSW TrainLink. It runs between Lithgow and Sydney in Australia, with a total distance of 156 kilometers. In 1958, it was operated by the New South Wales Government Railways using single-deck electric trains. Later on the operator was replaced by NSW TrainLink (double-deck electric trains) which uses double-deck electric trains.

The Coronation

The Coronation is an express passenger train that runs between London King's Cross and Edinburgh Waverley since July 5, 1937. Its name honored the coronation of King George VI and Queen Elizabeth. Its design was based on the The Silver Jubilee, a famous train built in 1935. At the rear of the train, a beaver tail-shaped observation car is available. During World War II The Coronation was discontinued and was preserved.

The Ghan

The Ghan is a passenger train that travels between Adelaide and Darwin in Australia. It was operated by Great Southern Rail and first entered service in 1929. Unfortunately, the original Ghan ran for the last time in 1980. However, in October this train was reintroduced to the public. The whole journey from Adelaide to Darwin is about 2,979 kilometers long and takes about 54 hours (4 hours stopover in Alice Springs included) for the Ghan to cover. Currently it operates twice a week from April to October and once a week on the remaining months.

The Gippslander

The Gippslander is a passenger train that travels from Melbourne to Bairnsdale via Gippsland region. It is operated by the Victorian Railways (railway company from Victoria, Australia) and runs from Monday to Saturday. It has a buffet car available from 1970s to 1980s. Today, The Gippslander name is still being used for regional trains that uses the same route. However, no special facilities like the buffet car are provided these days.

The Midlander

The Midlander is an Australian passenger train that runs between Rockhampton and Winton from 1954 to 1993. In 1935 the carriages were upgraded and became fully air-conditioned. The Midlander has dining cars, showers in the sleeping cars, and roomettes in first class accommodations. When tourism began to grow in western Queensland, especially at Longreach, the Midlander was renamed the Spirit of the Outback in November 1993. This new service then starts running from Brisbane to Longreach.

The Overland

The Overland is a passenger train that runs in Melbourne and Adelaide. It took its first ran in 1887 as the Adelaide Express. It was only in 1926 when it got its name "The Overland". Currently, it is being operated by Great Southern Rail, a private company. It runs twice a week in the 828 kilometers trips between Melbourne and Adelaide. Typically, the average journey time for a single trip takes 10 hours and 30 minutes.

The Red Dragon

The Red Dragon is an express passenger train operated by the Western Region of British Railways, a part of British Railways. It travels between London Paddington to Swansea and Carmarthen from 1950 to 1965. The Red Dragon also carried three different styles of headboard. The first one is in black or red with aluminum lettering. This particular headboard was introduced in 1951. In 1956, a new headboard style was briefly used – lighter background with dark painted letters. The third style, which is the most popular, was used from 1956 to 1962. The shape was a curved rectangle, painted in cream with brown letters. In the upper center, an image of a red dragon can be seen.

THSR 700T

The THSR 700T is a high speed train in Taiwan. It was first introduced in January 5, 2007 and travels between Taipei City and Kaohsiung. It has a top speed of 300 kilometers per hour and the whole journey between the two cities lasts for just 90 minutes. It is composed of 12 car sets. All these cars are soundproof and provide real time travel information. Though operating in Taiwan, this train was built in Japan by Kawasaki Heavy Industries, Nippon Sharyo and Hitachi. The 700T offers a business and standard seating classes. The business class can seat 66 passengers, while the standard class offers 923 seats.

TranzAlpine

The TranzAlpine is a passenger train operated by KiwiRail Scenic Journeys from New Zealand. It was considered as one of the world's great train journeys as it passes through breathtaking sceneries. The trip which is about 223 kilometers long between Christchurch and Greymouth takes about four hours and thirty minutes to cover. Additionally, the TranzAlpine also has on-board café, large windows, open-air carriage in middle of train and a baggage carriage.

Tren Crucero

The Tren Crucero is a first-class train that began service in 2014. It travels between Quito and Guayaquil in Ecuador on a 4 days and 3 nights journey. It also offers touring along the way and overnight stays in local hotels as it operates during daytime only. It is composed of four carriages – two dining cars and two lounge cars. The Tren Crucero also has a 54 seating capacity. It is indeed a wonderful way to see and experience the different landscapes of Ecuador.

Troop Sleeper

A troop sleeper is a railroad passenger car specifically built to serve as a mobile barracks when military troops are being transported over long distances. With this method, trips can be made overnight, hence, reducing the amount of journey time. During World War II, around 44 million armed services personnel were carried by troop sleepers. These railroad vehicles usually have end doors, wide side-doors, built-in trap doors and steps, ten window units on each side, rolling black out shades and wire mesh screens. Troop Sleepers were also generally equipped with beds stacked 3-high, complete with sheets and pillowcases that were changed daily. Moreover, Troop Sleepers came with two enclosed toilets and a drinking water cooler. Troop kitchens, are also fitted to provide meal service on-board. Though currently not in use Troop Sleepers are preserved in several railroad museums across the United States.

Twin Cities Hiawatha

The Twin Cities Hiawatha or Hiawatha is a passenger train that travels from Chicago to the Minneapolis. It was operated by the Chicago, Milwaukee, St. Paul and Pacific Railroad, a railroad company in the United States. It also got its name from the epic poem of Henry Wadsworth Longfellow titled, "The Song of Hiawatha". Originally, Hiawatha first ran in 1935, while in 1939, a second daily trip between Chicago and Minneapolis was introduced. The two trains were called, Morning Hiawatha and Afternoon Hiawatha. In 1970, the Afternoon Hiawatha was discontinued. The Morning Hiawatha on the other hand, continued its operation until 1971.

Venice Simplon-Orient-Express (VSOE)

The Venice Simplon-Orient-Express (VSOE) is a private luxury train owned by Belmond Ltd., a hotel and leisure company. It travels between London and Venice and other European cities. It was considered as the world's most authentic luxury train, with its restored vintage cars that dated back to the 1920s. The Venice Simplon-Orient-Express also has 12 sleeper cars, one bar car and offers five-star dining on its three dining cars.

Voralpen Express

The Voralpen-Express is a train operated since 1992 by Südostbahn (SOB), a railway company from Switzerland. It connects Lucerne and St. Gallen. The trains run every hour, with average journey time of 2 hours 15 minutes. In total, it has seven passenger coaches available in both First Class and Second Class seating. The First Class carriage differs from the Second Class carriage as it features a panorama view where passengers can fully enjoy and experience the beautiful scenery. The Voralpen-Express also has on-board vending machines where passengers can get foods and drinks.

Z-TER

The Z-TER is an electric regional passenger train or a train that runs between towns and cities of France. It was operated by SNCF and was manufactured by Alstom and Bombardier Transportation. It was also considered as the first regional train to attain a speed of 200 kilometer per hours. In total, there are 57 units built, all of which have three cars each and can only seat 211 passengers. Its overall length is about 79.20 meters, while the width and the height are around 2.905 meters and 4.218 meters respectively.

Images from: Tom Wigley, Derek Yu, Jim Duell, Dan Lundberg, Belur Ashok, André Marques, Nuno Morão, Gerry Zambonini, dhanur rananggono, Barry Lewis, Joshua Brown, Dennis Jarvis, Smeet Chowdhury, Lloyd, Chuck Taylor, ATSF104, Train Photos, Paul Sullivan, SounderBruce, David Tejera Gonzalez, Mark Evans, Clay Gilliland, Hugh Llewelyn, Simon Pielow, LHOON, yui.kubo, Blaise Machin, Marty Bernard, Loco Steve, nigelmenzies, Matthew Black, Daniel Luis Gómez Adenis, Rob Dammers, Alan Wilson, Liji Jinaraj, Kevan Dee, Kecko, Smudge 9000, pencroff, In Memory of Jim Pate II, calflier001, yisris, Kurt Haubrich, Markus Eigenheer, Simon Yeo, Clay Gilliland, Herry Lawford, fabian Pic´s, Bruce Fingerhood, ExactoCreation, 5th Luna, shankar s., David Wilson, Wolf Web, Chris Gladis, Train Photos, Don Graham, David Brossard, Martha de Jong-Lantink, Nelso Silva, Drew Jacksich, Ricardo Ricote Rodríguez, ERIC SALARD, Lars Steffens, unci_narynin, Bob Adams, Hec Tate, Roderick Eime, Andrew Bone, sundeviljeff, Whitevanman1024, Ryan McFarland, michaelgreenhill, Michael Coghlan, Barry Lewis, billy1125, mat79, Ministerio de Turismo Ecuador, vxla, Will Berghoff, Jeroen de Vries., SOB Suedostbahn, David McKelvey, /Flickr

Made in the USA
San Bernardino, CA
15 September 2017